Southern Lot

XMAS COLORING

CUTE & EASY COLORING BOOK

COLORING

LET YOUR IMAGINATION RUN WILD!

Coloring takes us to a world where freedom, creativity, and self-expression really pop, giving us a fun break from all the modern-day stress. It has not just become a relaxing activity but a must-have in our daily routine.

------ SHARE WITH US! --------

Your unique style makes every coloring page special. We'd love to see your creations! Drop some pictures with your feedback so we can enjoy the awesome work of a creative artist like you!

scan to join with us!

Southern Lotus

CONNECT WITH US

Please feel free to reach out to us if you have any questions.
coloring@southernlotus.com

CONNECT, SHARE and LEARN

FOLLOW us on Instargram

17:58
southernlotus.publishing
- Daily tutorials
- Coloring tips
- Free Artwork

Southern Lotus

@ southernlotus.publishing

Southern Lotus

Follow   Message

scan us for more fun!

Southern Lotus

Relaxing video!

Coloring tutorial!

A LITTLE NOTE BEFORE COLORING!

We select standard-quality paper to keep our products affordable due to the limited options available on Amazon. If you experience bleeding with certain pens or markers, placing a blank sheet of thicker paper behind the page can help. We are grateful for your understanding.

blank paper

THIS BOOK BELONGS TO

....

Ho ho ho!
Merry Christmas, my dear friend!

This year has not been easy for all of us, but you have made this world a better place with your kindness and love. Thank you so much for being with us throughout the past year. We hope that you will love the small surprises we have prepared for you.
Cherish every moment, and always remember that we carry you in our hearts.

With all our love and warm wishes!

Special gift for you: Scan the QR code to receive 3 FREE digital coloring books from our Xmas series!

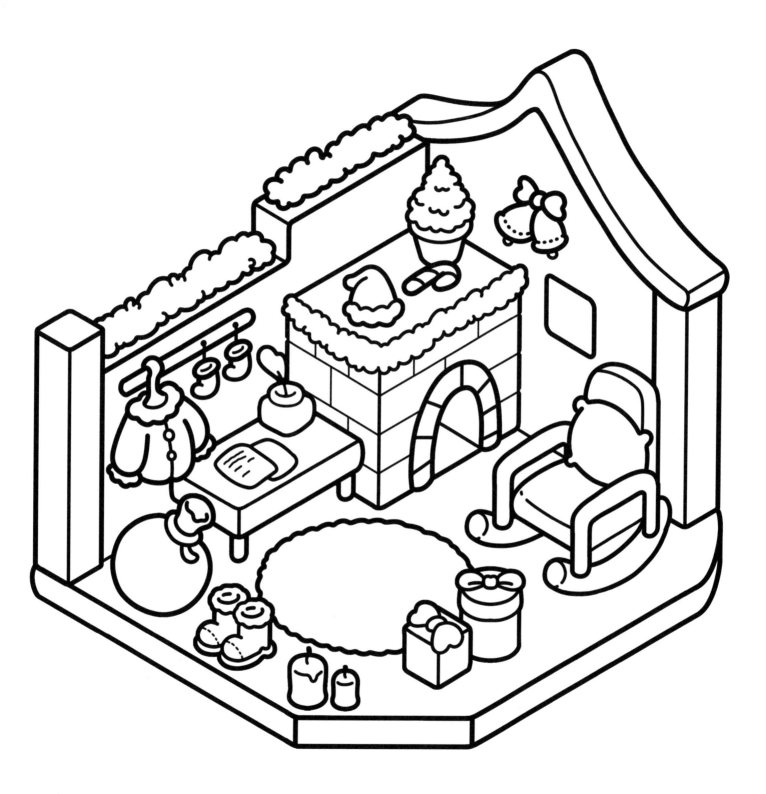

TEST COLOR PAGE

TEST COLOR PAGE

Use this paper underneath to prevent ink seepage and maintain the integrity of your creation (Optional)

BOLD AND EASY COLLECTION

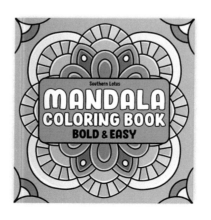

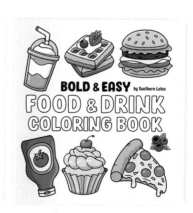

Made in the USA
Thornton, CO
11/01/24 17:02:08

c8cbf097-a372-4f02-a687-ec6c55a0f838R01